Rosie's new pet

Contents

Rosie's new pet

"No school next week, Joseph," said
Mrs Bates. "We're off to Planet X."

Joseph's mother was a reporter.
She often took Joseph to strange planets.

"Where's Planet X?" asked Joseph.

"Somewhere behind the moon," said
Mrs Bates. "Better take something warm."

They asked a friend to mind their pets
and caught the Monday morning rocket.

4

It only took a week to get to Planet X.

"Looks just like Earth," said Joseph, as they landed.

"It is," said his mother, "but without people. Planet X only has robots."

"That means no kids to play with," said Joseph, feeling sad.

"Never mind, you can watch TV in the motel," said Mrs Bates.

6

But Joseph couldn't find anything he liked on TV. His mother was busy talking on the phone and he felt bored. He looked out of the window. There was a park across the street.

"May I go to the park, Mum?" he asked.

"Okay," said Mrs Bates, "but don't go too far, and don't talk to strangers."

The park was just like any park at home, but it wasn't much fun on his own. Joseph sat on the grass and felt lonely. Just then, Rosie Robot came along.

"Poor little animal," she said. "You look lost!"

She picked Joseph up and walked off with him.

"Put me down!" yelled Joseph. "Put me down!"

But she couldn't hear him because of all the cars and lorries going by.

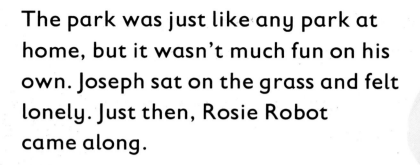

"Look what I found in the park," Rosie called when they got to her house.

Mr and Mrs Robot and Rosie's brother, Roger, came to look.

"What on earth is it?" said Mrs Robot.

"I'm a boy," said Joseph." Put me down!"

But they were so busy talking about
him that no one heard him.

"It's pink and white and blue," said Mrs Robot.

"It's got brown fur on its head," said Mr Robot.

"Does it bite?" asked Roger.

"Yes!" yelled Joseph.

But no one heard him. They were too
busy arguing about why his paws were different.

"It's got spots on its face," said Roger.

"I'm going to call it Spot," said Rosie.
"It can be my new pet."

"You can't call me Spot!" yelled Joseph.

But no one heard him.
They were too busy talking about what
a good name Spot was.

"I'm going to take Spot to school in the morning," said Rosie. "I'll show him to the class when I give my morning talk."

"I won't be part of a morning talk!" yelled Joseph, but Mrs Robot was busy telling them that it was time for tea, so no one heard him.

"Better give Spot some oil to drink," said Mr Robot.

"Don't let him make a mess," said Mrs Robot.

"Can he beg?" asked Roger.

"Boys don't beg," said Joseph.

But no one heard him. They were too busy crunching up their tea.

13

Joseph pushed his oil away.
"**I want a glass of water**!" he said loudly.

This time, everyone heard him.

"Water?" said Mrs Robot.

"Water?" said Mr Robot.

"Spot wants water!" said Roger.

"Oh no, Spot," said Rosie. "Water will make you all rusty inside."

"Boys don't get rusty!" yelled Joseph.

But no one heard him. They were too
busy arguing about what to watch on TV.

"Come on, Spot," said Rosie. "We're going
to watch Superman on TV. Then after the
show is over, you can come and sleep on
the end of my bed."

"Make sure his paws are clean before
you let him on your bed, Rosie," said Mrs Robot.

"I want to go back to my mother," said Joseph.
But no one heard him. They were too
busy arguing about where everyone was
going to sit.

Mr Robot turned on the TV.

"Here is a news flash," said the news robot. "It's about a lost human called Joseph Bates. He is visiting our planet with his mother. He was last seen going into the local park. If you know where he is, or if you have seen him anywhere, please call his mother at the Computer Motel."

"Hey, that's about me!" yelled Joseph.

"Quiet, Spot," said Mr Robot. "We're listening to the news flash."

"Here is a picture of Joseph Bates," said the news robot.

"Look, it's Spot!" cried Rosie and Roger together.

"So it is," said Mr Robot.

"Why didn't you tell us you were a human?" asked Mrs Robot.

"I did," said Joseph.

But no one heard him. They were too busy arguing about who would take him back to the motel.

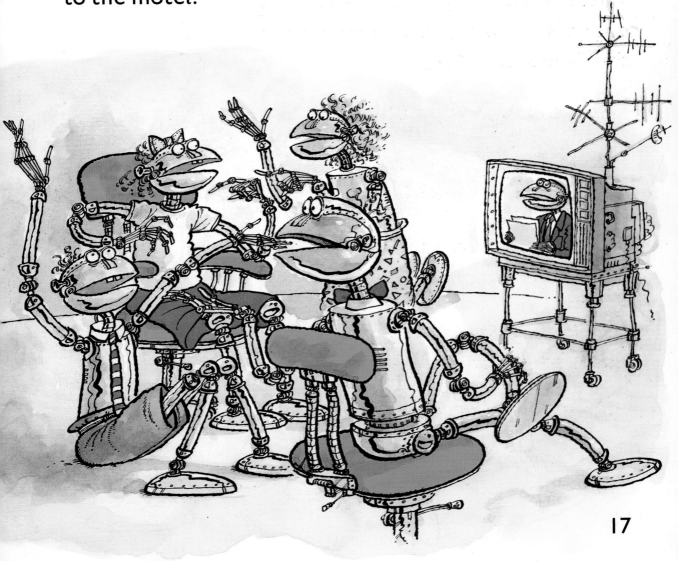

In the end, they all did.

"Goodbye," said Rosie, after they found Joseph's mother. "I'm sorry I can't take you to school for my morning talk."

"Would you like to?" asked Joseph.

"You bet," said Rosie. "No one else has ever taken a human."

"Okay," said Joseph, "I'll come."

19

Next day, Joseph went to school with Rosie.

"This is a human," Rosie told the class. "He is pink and white and blue and he has brown fur on his head. His top paws are different from his bottom paws and he doesn't get rusty when he drinks water. On Earth he is called Joseph Bates, but here on Planet X he's called Spot."

20

"I'm not!" yelled Joseph.

But no one heard him. They were much
too busy arguing about who was going to
pat him first.

21

My name is...

The monster from Mercury

Sally found the monster from Mercury at the bottom of their garden when she got home from school on Friday. It had just got out of a small spaceship.

"Dad won't like that," she said.
"Your spaceship is on top of his tomatoes."

"Where am I?" asked the monster.

"In our garden," said Sally.

"Is your garden on the moon?"
asked the monster.

"No," said Sally. "This is Earth."

25

"Then I'm lost," said the monster.
"I wonder where I went wrong. I must
have turned left instead of right when
I passed Mars. Or perhaps I went up
instead of down when I got to Venus.
What do you think?"

"I don't know," said Sally.
"I only know the way to school
and to the supermarket.
Where did you come from?"

"Mercury," said the monster.
"I should never have left.
Now I'll never find my way back."

It looked at Sally in a puzzled way.
"Why aren't you green?" it asked.

"Earth people aren't green,"
said Sally.

"They should be," said the monster.
It shut its eyes and said something quietly.
"There you are," it said, "that's better."

27

Sally looked at her hands.
They were green. Her arms were green
and her legs were green.
"Oh, my goodness!" she said.

She ran inside and looked in the mirror.
Sure enough, her face was green, too.
Even her hair was green.
Sally went back out to the monster.
"I don't think Mum will like it," she said.

"What's a mum?" asked the monster.

"She's ... she's ... "

Sally couldn't think what to say.
"I guess she's someone who looks after me,"
she said.

"Oh, your keeper," said the monster. "I see.
Well, I can soon fix that."

It shut its eyes and said something quietly.

"There you are," it said.
"Now she won't mind."

"Sally," called Sally's mother
from the front garden.
"Come and help me. I think I'm sick.
I was busy watering the flowers
and suddenly I turned all green."

"It's all right, Mum," Sally shouted.
"I'm green, too. Come and look."

Her mother came round the path.
"Why, so you are," she said.
"It must have been something we ate.
I thought those biscuits we had tasted funny."

"No, Mum," said Sally, "it wasn't the biscuits. The monster from Mercury did it."

Her mother saw the monster for the first time.

"Oh, my goodness," she said. "Where did that come from?"

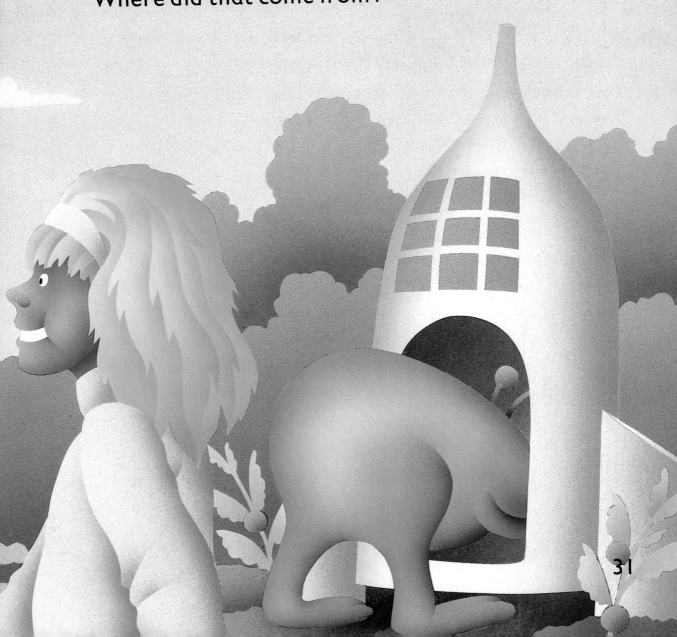

"From Mercury," said Sally.
"It got lost and landed in our garden."

"Right on top of the tomatoes," said her mother.
"Your father won't like that."

She went up to the monster.
"Now look here," she said crossly.
"You must stop this. We don't want
to be green."

"You look much nicer,"
said the monster.

32

"You might think so," said Sally's mother, "but we don't. Nobody on Earth is green."

The monster wasn't listening to her. It now had a pencil and a map and a calculator and it was trying to work something out.

"Let me see," it said. "Do I add or do I multiply?"

Sally and her mother went inside and sat down.
"Perhaps it will just go away, Mum," said Sally.
But it didn't.
And when Sally's brother, Bill, came home
from football practice, they were still green.

"Hey, that looks good," he said.
"Are you going to a party?"

"No," said his mother. "The monster from Mercury did it."

"It's out in the garden," said Sally, "with its spaceship."

"This I have to see," said Bill.

The monster looked up at Bill.
"Ugh," it said. "Another white one!"

It shut its eyes and said something quietly.
Right away, Bill turned green.
"That's better," said the monster.
Then it went back to its calculator.

It was the same when Sally's father came home.
And when the dog turned up looking for her tea,
the monster made her green, too.

"This has got to stop," said Sally's mother.

"Yes," said her father. "I'm not going to work on Monday looking like this! And what about my tomatoes?"

"I won't be allowed to play football if I'm green," grumbled Bill.

The dog hadn't noticed she was green. She was too busy wondering why no one had given her any tea.

The family went out into the garden. The monster was looking puzzled. "I just can't work it out," it grumbled. "I can't think where I'm going wrong."

"Let's have a look," said Bill.

The monster gave him the map and a piece of paper with lots of numbers written on it.

Sally thought the map looked like a road map,
only it had planets on it instead of towns.
"I have to work out how far it is
from Earth to Mercury," said the monster,
"but I keep going wrong."

Sally and Bill looked at the numbers
the monster had written down.
"That doesn't look right," said Bill suddenly.

"No," said Sally, "it's not."

She looked up at the monster.
"If we tell you the right answer
will you make us white again?"

"Don't you like being green?"
asked the monster in surprise.
"You look much nicer."

"We don't think so," said Sally.

"No," said her mother and father together. "We don't."

"Oh well," said the monster. "If that's what you want. Just let's get my map right, then I'll make you white again."

"Look," said Bill, "you made a mistake here.
That number should be 75 000 kilometres."

"Oh, of course," said the monster.
"What a silly mistake. Well, goodbye.
It's been nice meeting you."

It got into the spaceship.
"Wait!" shouted Sally's father. "You've
forgotten something. We're still green."

The monster shut its eyes and said
something quietly.

"There you are," it said, as it shut
the spaceship door. "Back to that awful
white again."
Then off it zoomed up into the sky.

"Just as well we're good at maths," said Sally.

"Woof!" said the dog, who was still
waiting for her tea.

"Oh no," said Sally's father. "We forgot her.
Now what do we do with a green dog?"

41

Lift-off!

Earthrise!

The little black train

There's a lit-tle black train a-com-ing,

Get all your busi-ness right,

There's a lit-tle black train a-com-ing,

And it may be here to-night.·····

Oh, the little black train is a-coming,
It's coming 'round the bend,
You can hear those wheels a-moving
And rattling through the land.

Or you could sing instead........

There's a big si-lver rocket a-go-ing,
Get all your busi-ness right,
There's a big si-lver ro-cket a-go-ing,
And it takes off to-night.

Oh, that big silver rocket's a-going,
Way, way out into space,
And you can zoom right off to Mars
Or any other far-off place.

Poems to act

The pirate chief

One-eyed Jack, the pirate chief,
   Was a terrible, fearsome ocean thief.
      He wore a peg
      Upon one leg;
      He wore a hook
      And a dirty look.
One-eyed Jack, the pirate chief,
A terrible, fearsome ocean thief.

Anon

The wicked burglar

Forth from his den to steal he stole,
   His bags of chink he chunk,
And many a wicked smile he smole,
   And many a wink he wunk.

Anon

The monster

I creep through children's bedrooms,
    I do it all the time,
For I'm a scary monster
    all oozy and drippy with slime.
I pounce on little babies
    and gobble them for my tea,
Their brothers' and sisters' tears and cries
    fill me with awful glee.
Watch out, watch out, wherever you go,
    I hide in cupboards, too,
And I decided late last night
    It's time that I ate
    YOU!

Pat Edwards